Vic   FEB 1 1 2011

D0031938

Officially
Withdrawn

ATOS Book Level: _____ 2.9 _____
AR Points: _____ 1.0 _____
Quiz #: 138695 ☑RP ☐ LS ☐ VP
Lexile: _____

Victorville City Library
15011 Circle Dr.
Victorville, CA 92395
760-245-4222

PATRICIA REILLY GIFF

Big Whopper

illustrated by

ALASDAIR BRIGHT

A YEARLING BOOK

Sale of this book without a front cover may be unauthorized. If the book is coverless, it may have been reported to the publisher as "unsold or destroyed" and neither the author nor the publisher may have received payment for it.

This is a work of fiction. Names, characters, places, and incidents either are the product of the author's imagination or are used fictitiously. Any resemblance to actual persons, living or dead, events, or locales is entirely coincidental.

Text copyright © 2010 by Patricia Reilly Giff
Illustrations copyright © 2010 by Alasdair Bright

All rights reserved. Published in the United States by Yearling, an imprint of Random House Children's Books, a division of Random House, Inc., New York. Simultaneously published in hardcover in the United States by Wendy Lamb Books, an imprint of Random House Children's Books, a division of Random House, Inc., New York.

Yearling and the jumping horse design are registered trademarks of Random House, Inc.

Visit us on the Web! www.randomhouse.com/kids

Educators and librarians, for a variety of teaching tools, visit us at www.randomhouse.com/teachers

Library of Congress Cataloging-in-Publication Data
Giff, Patricia Reilly.
Big whopper / Patricia Reilly Giff ; illustrated by Alasdair Bright. — 1st ed.
p. cm.
Summary: When Destiny Washington cannot think of a discovery during Discovery Week at school, she makes up a story but finds that she cannot keep on pretending it is true.
ISBN 978-0-385-74688-5 (trade) — ISBN 978-0-385-90926-6 (lib. bdg.)
ISBN 978-0-553-49469-3 (pbk.) — ISBN 978-0-375-89636-1 (e-book)
[1. Schools—Fiction. 2. Honesty—Fiction.] I. Bright, Alasdair, ill. II. Title.
PZ7.G3626Bi 2010
[Fic]—dc22
2009033020

Printed in the United States of America

10 9 8 7 6 5 4 3 2 1

First Yearling Edition

Random House Children's Books supports the First Amendment and celebrates the right to read.

Love to my favorite consultant,

Patti O'Meara

—P.R.G.

• • •

For B and John

—A.B.

Yolanda

Sumiko

Charlie

Destiny

Gina

Mitchell

Habib

Clifton

Trevor

Terrible
Thomas

Angel

Peter

CHAPTER 1

MONDAY

Everyone—kindergarten through sixth—stamped down the stairs. Destiny stamped, too.

It was time for the Afternoon Center at the Zelda A. Zigzag School.

Destiny Washington opened her mouth. "Hellooooo!" she called in her loudest voice.

It was a test. She really wasn't calling anyone. Except maybe her new friend Mitchell McCabe.

1

The test was to see if anyone could hear her.

The other kids were screaming, too. No one turned around. No one but Terrible Thomas.

Terrible Thomas was Jake the Sweeper's cat. He liked to sneak into the school. He ate the snacks that Jake's broom missed.

He liked to hiss, too.

The Afternoon Center took up most of the school's basement. It was a great place. The art room was down there. So was the lunchroom.

Destiny loved everything about the Center.

Dancing, and plays, art, and snack. She loved bouncing on the trampoline.

Gina raced along in front of Destiny. Her loopy pearl necklace swung back and forth. "Don't push!" she yelled. Her voice sounded like a jet plane.

Not only was she loud! She was bossy, too.

"Sorry," Destiny said.

Suddenly, a whistle blew. It was the screechiest noise Destiny had ever heard.

Everyone stopped yelling.

Everyone stopped stamping.

Destiny leaned over Gina's shoulder. What was going on?

"If you don't mind," Gina said.

Destiny stepped back. "Just trying to see."

Mrs. Farelli, the art teacher, stood at the bottom of the stairs. Her cheeks were as red as her whistle.

One of her arms was raised.

She looked like the Statue of Liberty. "Is this a herd of cattle?" she asked.

"Moooooo," Habib whispered.

"Humpf." Mrs. Farelli shook her head.

Destiny followed Gina into the lunchroom. Snack time was first.

Everything about the lunchroom was huge. Even the flowerpots on the windowsills.

Too bad the pots were full of dirt instead of flowers! They'd planted a bunch of seeds ages ago. But not one of them had popped up.

Destiny slung her backpack onto an empty lunch table.

"Listen up," Mrs. Farelli said.

Uh-oh, Destiny thought. They were in trouble.

Mrs. Farelli leaned forward. "Afternoon Center boys and girls don't stampede down the stairs. They don't push each other."

Destiny made herself as small as she could. Did Mrs. Farelli mean her?

"Afternoon Center boys and girls don't moo," Mrs. Farelli said.

That was definitely Habib, Destiny thought. He ducked in back of Mitchell McCabe.

Mrs. Farelli could probably see him anyway. She said she could see through walls.

"Be kind," Mrs. Farelli said. "That's the way we do things at the Afternoon Center."

"That's me," Gina said. She looped her fingers around her pearls. "Kind!"

"Humpf," Destiny said.

"Here's some exciting news," Mrs. Farelli said.

Something exciting was always happening at the Afternoon Center. Destiny tried to hear.

Gina was humming opera. She sang, "*La donna mobile home...*"

Habib was juggling with one apple.

Trevor, one of the kindergarten kids, was reading a book upside down. He was making up the words.

His friend Clifton was listening. He was making up words, too.

Mrs. Farelli reached for her whistle. *Brrrrrrr!*

"This is Discovery Week," Mrs. Farelli said, when everyone stopped holding their ears.

"I like to discover new things," said Gina.

"We'll discover things all week," Mrs. Farelli said. "Anything you see or learn for the first time counts."

"I'll be great at this," Gina said.

Destiny wanted to say *humpf.* She didn't, though. That wasn't the way they did things at the Zelda A. Zigzag Afternoon Center.

Mrs. Farelli twirled her whistle. "The best part is—"

Destiny held her breath.

"—on Thursday, we'll take a bus. We'll visit the Discovery Museum." Mrs. Farelli was smiling.

An after-school trip, Destiny thought. *Cool!*

She was lucky her mom was a hairdresser. Her mom would do something special with her hair. She'd lend Destiny neon green nail polish.

Destiny would look spectacular!

In the meantime, she'd have to discover something.

But what?

She thought of Christopher Columbus.

There was no land left to discover.

She thought of the guy who discovered light-bulbs. Destiny had plenty of light in her house.

Maybe there wasn't anything new left.

Humpf!

CHAPTER 2

STILL MONDAY

What was that?

A blast of noise.

Rattling!

Everyone raced out to the basement hall.

"Out of my way!" Gina screeched.

Habib was juggling with one apple. "Be careful!" he yelled. "This apple is mostly mush."

Destiny didn't waste time screeching or

yelling. She ducked around Mitchell. She slid around Charlie. She hopped over Terrible Thomas.

Thomas swished his tail back and forth at her.

Ellie and Ramón, the college helpers, were zigzagging down the hall.

They pushed a giant cart.

The wheels galumphed.

A huge roll of paper clunked back and forth on top.

"This is Discovery Week," Ellie shouted. Her ponytail zipped around behind her.

"Get aboard," yelled Ramón. He waved his baseball cap.

A bunch of kids hopped onto the cart.

Destiny and her friend Sumiko ran together. Sumiko even did an almost-cartwheel. She was great at gym.

Mitchell and Habib ran with them to the end of the hall.

The cart banged into the wall.

"Yeow!" Ellie said.

"Double yeow!" Destiny sank down on the edge of the cart. Discovery Week was fun. Especially when you didn't have to think of discoveries.

"Here comes the hard part," Ramón said.

Destiny looked at the roll of white paper. It was as big as an elephant.

But Ramón was as big as an elephant, too.

She watched him wrestle the roll off the cart.

Ellie held out a box of pushpins. "We're going to roll this paper across the wall . . . all the way back down the hall."

"Won't it cover the doors?" Destiny asked. What if Mrs. Farelli couldn't get into the art room? She'd have another fit.

Besides, what was this paper stuff all about?

"Don't worry." Ellie made cutting motions with her fingers. "We'll make doorways."

Ms. Katz came down the stairs. "Super work," she said. "And all for Discovery Week. We'll list our discoveries on paper."

Destiny helped Ramón unroll the paper.

It slipped away from them.

It rolled halfway down the hall.

Terrible Thomas raced ahead of it. He disappeared into the mop closet.

The roll of paper stopped by itself.

"Now," Ramón said. "We'll tack this up along the wall."

It won't be easy, Destiny thought.

Everyone held part of the paper.

Ramón tacked it up.

It was more fun than coming up with a discovery.

When the paper was up, it was full of:

Apple mush.

Footprints.

A lump of someone's cheese popper.

A smear of pizza from snack time.

**Something pink. Maybe Ellie's lip
     gloss?**

Chocolate.

"Whew," Destiny said.

"Yuck," Gina said.

"I think I see some of your cheese popper, Gina," Sumiko said. But she said it kindly. She did one more cartwheel in front of Gina.

Charlie pointed to a spot. "That's from my chocolate nutto bar," he said.

"Never mind," Ellie said. "No one will notice."

Ms. Katz handed out a pile of markers. "Mrs. Farelli said it was all right to use these. But don't make a mess on the floor."

Destiny nodded. Jake the Sweeper would have a fit, too, if they made a mess.

Lots of fits going around, she thought, and smiled to herself.

Ramón brought benches for everyone to stand on.

"Put your names up there. Leave plenty of room for your discoveries."

"I'm in luck," Yolanda said. "I just discovered how to draw with markers."

Gina stood up on the bench next to Destiny. "You'd better move over." Gina made a gigantic circle in the air with her marker. "I need room. I'm great at discovering things."

Destiny moved over. She didn't think she needed plenty of room. She didn't need any room at all.

She didn't have one idea for a discovery.

CHAPTER 3

TUESDAY

Destiny stopped at the bottom of the stairs.

The not-so-white paper stretched from one end of the basement hall to the other. Doorways were snipped out.

People had begun to write their discoveries on the paper. Destiny read what Charlie had to say:

I made a magnet once.
It was a great discovery.
I forget how.
If I remember, I'll write it down.

Destiny wished she could think of a discovery she'd forgotten!

She read Gina's next.

When a singer hits a high note, her
  voice WIGGLES.
Her high note can break a glass.
I found out I can break a glass, too.

Lucky Gina.

Destiny sang like a crow.

If only she could think of something like . . .

How to make a rocket ship. It would blast off from the schoolyard, right into space.

Destiny snapped her fingers. How about the guy who came up with earplugs? Your ears stayed dry as a bone when you went swimming.

Everybody thought that was terrific.

A little thing like earplugs!

If only she had thought of it first.

Right now, Mitchell was writing.

Destiny leaned forward to see.

He crossed it out.

"I know how to make a bell ringer," he said. "But I just remembered. Someone did that already."

"That's the whole problem," Destiny said. "There's nothing left to discover."

She waved at Mitchell. Then she climbed down and ducked into the girls' room.

She leaned toward the mirror. Her nose almost touched the glass. Her eyes crossed.

Today she had a purple stripe in her hair. Her mother had sprayed it on last night.

What could be better?

She wasn't going to think about discoveries right now. Today was filled with good things.

She was going straight to the art room.

In the hall, Trevor, a kindergarten kid, was

sitting on Mr. Oakley's shoulders.

Mr. Oakley was a grandfather. He helped out at the Center. "Hurry," he told Trevor. "You're a big guy. I'm going to sink."

"One more second." Trevor reached up. He began to write on the wall.

Destiny stopped to see what he'd write.

It was only a bunch of letters.

Trevor looked down at Destiny. "I wrote about my discovery. I can make sparks. I wave my blanket around in the dark."

"Wave yourself off my shoulders, please," said Mr. Oakley.

"Me next," said Clifton.

"All right," Mr. Oakley said.

"Never mind," Clifton said. "I've never discovered anything in my life."

Destiny nodded. "Me neither."

Destiny hurried toward the art room. Everyone else hurried, too. They were going to the gym, or outdoors to the nature center, or to the lunchroom for snack.

Wait a minute!

Snack. She had almost forgotten.

She rushed to the lunchroom.

The lunch lady was giving out chocolate pudding in little cups. Or vanilla.

Destiny hurried past the flowerpots that were full of dirt. No flowers!

She stood next to the lunch lady. She liked to help with snacks.

The lunch lady was tall and round. She wore a shower cap on her head. Her ears stuck out.

She looked like a doughnut.

A nice sugary doughnut.

"I'll give out the pudding, too," Destiny said.

"Whew," said the lunch lady. "That will help."

Destiny smiled. She felt sugary inside, too.

She gave chocolate pudding to Mitchell and Habib.

They were good friends.

She gave two chocolate pudding cups to Sumiko.

That was only fair. Sumiko was learning Japanese from her mother and father. Her brain needed lots of vitamins. So did the rest of her. She wanted to be a gymnast when she grew up.

"*Arigato,*" Sumiko said. "That means 'thank you.'"

Destiny gave a plain vanilla pudding to Gina.

That was only fair, too. Gina had a pearl necklace. Besides, she didn't deserve chocolate. She was going around breaking glasses with her wiggly voice.

Mr. Randolph, the principal, came along.

Destiny gave him the biggest pudding on the tray.

She reached for a chocolate one for herself.

And that was fair, too. She had helped the lunch lady. Destiny licked her spoon, back and front.

Then she headed for the art room.

Right now, Ms. Katz was in charge of art. That was because Mrs. Farelli wanted to go home after the bell rang this week. "Enough school is enough," Mrs. Farelli had said.

Great! Ms. Katz was one of Destiny's best friends. That was if you counted grown-ups.

Destiny knew a lot about Ms. Katz. Her first name was Vivian.

But something else. Ms. Katz wasn't glamorous.

She didn't polish her nails.

And her hair! Plain brown.

Sometimes she wore glasses. They were plain, too. Poor Ms. Katz.

She should give orange or purple hair a try.

Habib walked in front of Destiny. He was juggling with one apple again. An almost-rotten apple.

"Great purple hair," he told her.

He didn't wait for her to say thanks. His apple had just thumped away.

He ran to catch up with it.

Apple mush was all over the stairs. All that was left of the apple was the core.

Destiny jumped over the mess.

She stopped at the art room.

Terrible Thomas was curled up in front of the door. He was fat. And sleepy.

"Excuse me," Destiny told him. "How did you get in here again?"

She leaned over him and opened the door.

The room was filled.

Every seat was taken.

"No room." Gina waved her necklace around. "Try something else today."

That Gina!

Humpf!

CHAPTER 4

STILL TUESDAY

Destiny bit her lip. She loved art.

You could work with paper—all different colors, even purple. Just like her hair stripe.

There were paper clips and doilies.

Scissors and crayons.

Pipe cleaners and—

Just everything in the world for art.

Sumiko slid over in her seat. "We can share."

"You saved my life," Destiny said.

"Lovely," Ms. Katz told Sumiko.

Lovely was Ms. Katz's favorite word.

Gina looked up. "I was going to give Destiny my seat," she said.

Ms. Katz tapped her lip. "Someone could sit at my desk."

Gina was up in a flash. "You can have my seat," she told Destiny.

Destiny was just as fast. They raced to the front. They slid into Ms. Katz's chair at the same time.

"Good sharing," Ms. Katz said.

But Gina was taking up the whole seat.

Destiny held on to Ms. Katz's desk. She tried to give Gina a tiny push.

No good. Humpf! That Gina was as strong as a coyote.

Then Destiny had an idea. "I'll give things out to everyone."

"Me too," said Gina.

Gina raced to the closet ahead of Destiny. She began to slap stuff on tables.

She was making a big mess. Crayons were rolling around. Paper clips flew all over the place.

Destiny tried to be neater.

She gave Charlie brand-new markers.

She gave Angel a pack of pipe cleaners.

She put a thick piece of paper on her half of the desk.

It was purple, her favorite color.

She put pointy colored pencils on top of it.

But she didn't sit down. She watched Habib and Mitchell. They were making clay robots.

The robot heads looked squashed.

Sumiko was drawing a cherry tree. "My mother said cherry trees are very Japanese."

It didn't look exactly like a cherry tree. It was more like a Christmas tree with pink ornaments.

"Lovely," Destiny said in a Ms. Katz voice.

Ms. Katz was standing next to her desk.

Ms. Vivian Katz with her plain brown hair and no-nail-polish fingers.

Poor Ms. Katz.

Destiny tried to give her a hint. "My mother works at Cut and Curl," she said.

Ms. Katz smiled.

"You'd look great with blue hair," Destiny said. "To match your eyes."

She didn't have time to say anything else.

Gina was listening.

Destiny slid into her half-seat.

She spread out her paper. It was a little on Gina's space.

It was a big piece of paper, after all.

What could she draw?

A flower?

Everyone drew flowers.

A picture of the Zelda A. Zigzag School?

Too hard.

Habib juggling an apple?

Habib would be thrilled.

She drew a nice long body and a skinny head.

It actually didn't look like Habib.

It looked more like an old man.

All right. She'd make a wizard.

Did wizards have beards? Yes. She gave him a nice black beard.

Gina's elbow was sticking out over the wizard's foot.

Destiny didn't bang her own elbow into Gina's. That was not the way they did things at the Zelda A. Zigzag Afternoon Center.

She took a peek at Gina's side of Ms. Katz's desk. Gina had cut up bits of shiny paper. She was pasting them to a black piece of paper.

It was better than anything Destiny could ever do.

She thought about what Mrs. Farelli had said.

"That's nice artwork," she made herself say.

"I know." Gina frowned. She pointed at the wizard. "What's that?"

Destiny looked down at her picture.

It was a *humpf* drawing.

Her wizard's feet looked like horses' hooves. The legs looked like pipe cleaners.

He didn't look one bit like a wizard.

What did he look like?

She had to think fast. "It's a president."

"It doesn't look like any president I know," Gina said.

Destiny's mouth flew open. The words came out before she could stop them. "Do you remember my last name?"

Gina raised her shoulders in the air. "Destiny Washington, everyone knows that. Just like I'm Gina Maria Arlia."

"Yes, Destiny Washington." She said the *Washington* part loud. "That's because my great-great-greatest-grandfather was President Washington. The Father of Our Country."

Now Gina's mouth flew open.

Destiny wrote on top of her paper:

**ABREHEM WASHINGTON
FATHER OF OUR KUNTRY
MY GREATEST
GREAT GRENDFATHER**

Gina didn't look. She bent over her gorgeous cutout drawing. She didn't say another word.

Good, Destiny thought. Then she swallowed. Telling fibs was not the way they did things at the Zelda A. Zigzag Afternoon Center.

CHAPTER 5

WEDNESDAY

Yesterday, Tuesday, was Mrs. Washington's day off.

She was there when Destiny got off the bus. "What's the matter, cookie?" she asked.

Destiny couldn't tell her.

What would Mom think of her Abraham Washington picture?

What would she think of Destiny's fib?

Destiny's grand-fathers certainly weren't presidents.

One was a taxi driver.

The other one stayed home and read the newspapers.

"I'll do your hair," Destiny's mother said. "Want me to trim your bangs?"

Destiny thought of her picture on the purple paper.

Purple wasn't her favorite color anymore.

It was the worst color in the world.

Today she had hated going to school.

All day long something had rolled around in her head.

What was it?

At the end of the day she had remembered.

Oh, no!

Abraham Washington was still on the desk in the art room.

Destiny had told Mitchell all about it on the way to Afternoon Center.

"Wow," Mitchell said. "You told a whopper!" He bit his nail. He looked at the ceiling.

That was what he did when he was figuring things out.

"Are you sure Abraham Washington wasn't your greatest-grandfather?" he asked.

"I don't think so," Destiny said. "My grandfather would have told me. He talks a lot when he's not reading the newspapers."

Mitchell bobbed his head up and down.

"Maybe we should try to get the picture back," he said. "Tear it into a thousand pieces. Put it in the lunchroom basket with the noodles and gravy."

Destiny nodded.

Mitchell was a good friend. But more than that. He was a thinker.

"We have to be first in the art room," he said.

They began to run. They skidded down the stairs. They raced along the hall. They passed the not-so-white discovery paper.

No one was in the art room except Terrible Thomas. He was curled up on the teacher's desk.

And there was the picture underneath Thomas.

"I can breathe again," Destiny said.

"Watch out for Thomas," Mitchell said. "He's a scratcher."

Destiny reached out carefully. She gave Thomas a tiny pat. "You're not supposed to be here," she said.

Thomas closed his eyes.

Slowly, Destiny pulled the drawing out from under Thomas. Very slowly.

Mitchell looked at it. He began to laugh. "Didn't President Washington have white hair? Kind of curly?"

"You're right!" Destiny put her hand up to her mouth. "Wait a minute. Wasn't his name George?"

Mitchell opened his eyes wide. "Abraham was someone else. Abraham Lincoln."

"He was the one with the black beard," Destiny said.

This was getting worse and worse.

It was a whole mixed-up picture.

One huge whopper.

Destiny was ready to rip it to shreds.

But the door opened.

It was Mrs. Farelli.

"What are you doing in here?" she asked.

"I just came to get my drawing," Destiny said.

"Humpf," said Mrs. Farelli. "Wait until Ms. Katz gets here for that."

Destiny's mouth went dry. "I just—"

"It's snack time," said Mrs. Farelli. "You'd better hurry. There might not be anything left."

Destiny could hear the noise in the hall. Everyone was running back and forth.

She put her drawing back on the desk.

Mrs. Farelli shooed Terrible Thomas out the door. Then she waited until Destiny and Mitchell went into the hall.

They walked slowly.

Lots of people were writing discoveries.

"Look at mine," Habib said.

I'm a juggler.
I drop an apple.
I drop a ball at the same time.
The apple is heavier.
They still get to the ground
     together.
This is really my dad's discovery.

"Neat," Mitchell said.

Destiny nodded. "That's really good, Habib."

"You look sad," Habib told her.

He was right. She was thinking about Ms. Katz.

Ms. Katz with her plain brown hair and no-polish nails.

Ms. Katz, who said *lovely* every two minutes.

Ms. Katz, who would see her Abraham Washington drawing.

She'd know Destiny had told a whopper.

How disappointed she'd be.

CHAPTER 6

STILL WEDNESDAY

"Let's stop in the lunchroom for snack," Mitchell said. "Then I have to go to Homework Help."

Destiny nodded. But she was never going to eat again.

The lunch lady was standing up in front. Destiny wished she could tell her what had gone wrong. But she couldn't do that, either.

Bags of dried pine-
apple were stacked up on
the lunch tables.

No one wanted to try
dried pineapple. No one
but Destiny.

"Eeew," Gina said.
"Disgusting."

Destiny looked at the
lunch lady.

The lunch lady looked a little sad.

Did grown-ups feel sad, too?

Destiny shook her head at Gina. "The lunch
lady tries to give us healthy snacks," she said.

Gina put her nose up close to Destiny. "Then
why don't you take one?"

Destiny made herself take a bag of dried
pineapple. She tried to find a teensy piece inside.

She put it in her mouth.

She was too sad to swallow.

She chewed a little. A surprise! The pineapple tasted sweet.

"It's good," she said.

"That's my girl," said the lunchroom lady.

Destiny took another piece. She closed her eyes.

It made her feel better.

Then Sumiko and Mitchell took a bag.

"*Ti,*" Sumiko said. "That's 'nice' in Japanese."

"We have to try things at the Afternoon Center," Destiny said. She didn't exactly say it to Gina. She said it to the air.

She wanted to be a good Afternoon Center person . . . even if they put her out for telling whoppers.

Everyone was leaving the lunchroom now.

Maybe she could still be first in the art room.

"Hurry," Mitchell whispered.

Destiny knew he was thinking the same thing. She began to slide out of the lunchroom.

But the lunchroom lady clapped her hands. "Destiny. Destiny Washington."

Destiny walked back slowly. "Did you call me?"

Everyone else was gone now.

The lunchroom lady patted a seat at a table. "Sit a minute," she said.

Destiny sat down. She thought about taking another bag of pineapple.

She didn't, though.

She was ready to cry. She'd never get Abraham Washington back before Ms. Katz saw it.

"I like your bangs," the lunch lady said.

"Thank you," Destiny said.

"It was very nice of you to try the pineapple," the lunch lady said.

"Thank you," Destiny whispered.

"So what's wrong? You can tell me."

Destiny looked toward the doorway. Mitchell was waiting for her.

So was Sumiko. She was doing a handstand.

"Nothing's wrong." Destiny's eyes burned.

The lunch lady was smiling a little. "When something is wrong, I cook up some turnips."

"Do you like turnips?" Destiny asked.

"Of course not," the lunch lady said. "I make

myself take a bite. I tell myself, 'Violet, things could be worse. You could have to eat turnips every day.'"

Destiny had to smile. She'd just learned the lunch lady's name. Violet. Neat.

"Good," said the lunch lady. "Now tell me what's the matter."

Destiny couldn't tell about the picture.

What else was wrong?

"I haven't discovered anything," she said.

That was true.

"I'll be the only one with a blank space on the wall."

That was true, too.

Now she felt even worse.

"That's not so ter-rible," the lunch lady said. "You discov-ered you like dried pineapple."

"That's not a great discovery," Destiny said.

The lunch lady laughed. "Come over to the windowsill."

They looked at the row of pots together.

"Do you see that?" the lunch lady said.

All Destiny saw was brown dirt.

The lunch lady pointed.

A tiny green shoot was poking up its head.

"See," said the lunch lady. "You've discovered a new plant."

"I guess," said Destiny.

"Just keep your eyes open," the lunchroom lady said. "You'll make a ton of discoveries."

Destiny nodded. If only she could believe her!

She ran to catch up with Mitchell and Sumiko.

CHAPTER 7

STILL WEDNESDAY

They reached the art room out of breath.

Three seats were left.

"That was *koun*," Sumiko said. "That means 'good luck' in Japanese."

But Ms. Katz was wearing a jacket. "Let's go outside," she said. "Bring paper. Bring colored pencils. We'll draw in the schoolyard."

Everyone raced for the door. They didn't even need jackets. It was warm out.

Great for sitting on the benches.

Over their heads were a million trees.

Well, maybe not a million.

But they were all different colors. Red, and yellow, and orange.

It was fall, after all.

Destiny put her backpack on the bench next to her.

She wanted to save space for Mitchell.

Terrible Thomas jumped up onto the table.

Destiny rubbed his ear.

She listened. Maybe he'd purr.

He didn't.

Thomas was an irritable cat.

Now Gina walked around. She twirled her pearl necklace.

She was looking for a seat. All the benches were taken.

Humpf! Gina was a pain.

But still—

Destiny scrunched over. She saved a teensy bit less of the bench for Mitchell, too.

"You can sit here," she told Gina.

Gina plopped herself down.

She took up a lot of room.

Mitchell dashed outside. He squeezed onto the one inch of bench.

He grinned at Destiny. "I have news. It's about something that belongs to you."

"What's that?" Gina asked.

Mitchell wiggled his nose at her.

Destiny knew what he meant. He was telling Gina not to be nosey.

He leaned closer to Destiny. "I dumped your drawing," he whispered. "It's in with the noodles and gravy."

Destiny sat back. Whew!

She didn't sit back for long.

Gina was staring at her. "Can you put two discoveries up on the board?" she asked.

Destiny thought about it.

But while she was thinking, Ms. Katz came along. "These trees are lovely." She waved her no-nail-polish hands around.

"Yes," Destiny said. The whole world was lovely now that she didn't have to worry about Abraham Washington.

She looked at the school windows.

Some kids were swinging on the gym ropes.

In the auditorium, some kids were working on a play.

A book club was meeting in the library.

Destiny loved the Afternoon Center.

She loved everyone.

Gina was still looking at her.

What was that all about?

Destiny picked up a pencil.

She began to draw a tree. She made a nice round ball of leaves on top.

She thought about the plant that had discovered how to grow.

She picked up a green pencil.

She drew a small plant next to the tree.

Gina poked her elbow into Destiny's side.

"Hey," Destiny said.

"Sorry," Gina said.

Did she really sound sorry? Destiny wasn't sure.

"I wanted to ask you," Gina said again. "Can you write two discoveries on the board?"

Two discoveries!

"I guess so," Destiny said.

Gina began to sing. *"La-da-dee-da."* She stopped. "The discovery is about you."

Destiny took a breath.

It must be about the Abraham Washington picture!

Gina was going to tell everyone in the Zelda A. Zigzag School about her whopper.

It would be on the discovery wall for everyone to see!

CHAPTER 8

THURSDAY

It was trip day at last.

Destiny's hair was piled up on her head. It was in a puff with a pink ribbon.

She stopped at the not-so-white paper wall.

A sixth grader named Peter Petway had written a discovery.

It had something to do with numbers. They were squeezed in all over the place.

Destiny passed her own blank space.

It was the only clean spot on the whole wall.

Mitchell and Habib were standing there. "We did one together," Mitchell said. "It's discovering how to make a parachute."

Tie string on 4 corners of a paper.
Knot the strings together.
Stick a robot on the end.
Throw it out the window.

"Does that work?" Destiny asked.

"Why not?" said Habib. "We're going to try it tomorrow. You can watch."

"Cool." If only she could think up something.

It was time to go to the bus.

No one pushed.

No one stomped.

Everyone handed in their permission slips

quietly. That was because strict Mrs. Farelli was going with them.

Ms. Katz was there, too. She was at the back of the bus. She was singing with the fifth graders.

Destiny slid into a seat next to Sumiko.

"That's *koun* for me," Destiny said.

Sumiko smiled. "You remembered it means 'good luck.'"

Mitchell sat in front with Habib.

Mitchell's sister, Angel, was squished in with Mrs. Farelli.

"Lucky we're together," Destiny whispered to Sumiko.

"*Hai,*" Sumiko said. "Yes."

The trip was fast. In two minutes the bus pulled into the parking lot.

Mrs. Farelli marched to the front. "Remember," she said. "Afternoon Center people don't run around like coyotes."

"Ruff ruff," Habib whispered.

Outside the bus, Mrs. Farelli counted everyone. "Two by two," she said. "Like Noah's Ark."

Destiny and Sumiko smiled at each other. They were going to be partners.

But wait a minute! Something wasn't working out right.

Charlie was ahead of them. He was walking by himself.

"*Ak'un,*" Sumiko said. "Bad luck!"

"Double *ak'un,*" said Destiny.

Sumiko and Charlie had to be partners.

Destiny twirled around.

Gina was marching along behind her. "We're partners," Gina said.

"Stick to your partners like glue," Mrs. Farelli called after them.

"Let's go to the gift store first," Gina said.

She waved a dollar in the air.

Destiny felt her pockets.

They were both empty. She had forgotten her money!

She tried to think of something else to do. "Let's go into the Discover the Heart and Lung room," she said. "We can walk right inside a heart."

"Whose heart?" Gina asked. She had a pile of quarters in her hand.

"Nobody's heart," Destiny said. "It's made out of plastic."

"Borrrrring," Gina said. "Let's head for the store. I have all this money to spend."

Sumiko and Charlie were up ahead. They were going to the Discover Japan room.

"Let's—" Destiny began.

But Gina didn't wait. "I know someplace else we can go first," she said.

Destiny followed her. She saw the sign. DISCOVER THE PRESIDENTS.

"You can even see their pictures," Gina said.

Destiny felt her own heart thumping. "Let's go somewhere else."

Gina turned. "I guess this is borrrrring for you."

What was Gina talking about?

"You know all about the presidents," Gina said. "Just think about your greatest-grandfather."

Destiny swallowed. "You said you knew something about me. For the not-so-white discovery board."

"Yes." Gina slid onto a bench outside the presidents room. "You're a good Afternoon Center person."

"Really?" Destiny said.

Gina nodded. "You tried the pineapple. You gave me a seat on the bench." She made a face. "A little piece of seat. But even so."

Destiny looked into the presidents room. She saw a statue of George Washington. And another of Abraham Lincoln.

She thought about being a good Afternoon Center person.

Ms. Katz was coming down the hall toward them.

She knew she had to tell the truth. No matter what.

It was the way they did things at the Zelda A. Zigzag Afternoon Center.

CHAPTER 9

STILL THURSDAY

Destiny could hardly breathe.

Ms. Katz stopped in front of them.

"My greatest-grandfather wasn't President Washington," Destiny said.

Gina's mouth opened. "He wasn't?"

Ms. Katz's mouth opened, too. "Is that what you said?"

Ms. Katz sank down on the bench next to

Gina. "You'd better sit down, too," she told
Destiny.

"You told a whopper," Gina said.

Destiny began to cry. "I'm sorry," she said.

Gina began to cry, too.

That Gina. Why was she crying?

"I told a whopper, too," Gina said. "I even wrote it on the not-so-white-paper wall."

Ms. Katz tilted her head.

"I can't break a glass when I sing," Gina said. "Only when it falls off the table. By accident."

Destiny sniffled. "That's a whopper."

Ms. Katz put one arm around Destiny. She put the other arm around Gina. "It's easier to tell the truth. That way your stomach doesn't get tied in knots."

Destiny nodded. So did Gina.

Destiny looked up at Ms. Katz's plain brown hair. She looked at her no-polish nails. But most of all, she looked at Ms. Katz's face.

She had just discovered something.

Ms. Katz didn't need lip gloss, or nail polish. She was gorgeous anyway.

Ms. Katz stood up. Something was happening to her face.

What?

"Is she trying not to laugh?" Gina whispered.

Destiny wasn't sure. But one thing she knew. Ms. Katz wasn't angry.

And another thing. Destiny was never going to tell another whopper. Even when she was forty years old.

"Come on," Ms. Katz said. "Let's learn about discoveries."

Destiny stood up. So did Gina.

They went into a room. It was dark as night. Ms. Katz gave them a map. "Look up at the ceiling," she said. "Can you see the stars?"

Destiny didn't look up. She flapped her jacket around in the dark. Trevor was right.

Sparks!

Next they went to the presidents room to discover some presidents. After that, they walked inside a huge heart.

What a discovery! It didn't look one bit like a Valentine heart.

But best of all, they went to the gift store.
Gina lent Destiny a dollar.

Destiny bought a book about the presidents.
President Washington's picture was right on
the front!

CHAPTER 10

FRIDAY

Everyone crowded into an upstairs classroom with Ms. Katz and Mrs. Farelli.

Ms. Katz opened the window.

"Are you ready?" Mitchell yelled.

"Ready," everyone called back.

Destiny began to count: "One. Two. Three. Go!"

"Goodbye, robot," Habib said.

He and Mitchell tossed the parachute out the window.

It sailed outside—

And got caught in the oak tree.

"Wack!" Habib yelled.

"Good try," Ms. Katz said.

"That's the way it works with discoveries," Mrs. Farelli said. "Some turn out better than others."

Destiny took a breath. She was going to write in her discovery space at last.

She skipped out of the room. She was still thinking.

She went downstairs.

She heard a noise.

The mop closet door was open a tiny bit.

She looked inside. Her mouth flew open.

She stood there for a few minutes, smiling.

Everyone else was coming downstairs now.

They had last-minute things to write before Discovery Week was over.

Gina crossed out her breaking-the-glass discovery. She put in something about Destiny.

It was too messy to read.

"Sorry," Gina said. "It's good, though."

Sumiko wrote:

My new word is _hakken_.
That means "discovery."

Mitchell went next:

Sometimes parachutes go bonk!

Then Destiny began to write in her own space.

First she put down two things she had discovered about presidents:

George Washington had curly white
**   hair.**

Abraham Lincoln had a bumpy nose.

"Don't forget Franklin Obama," Mitchell said.

That doesn't sound right, Destiny thought.

"It's Barack Obama," Mitchell said.

"That sounds right," Destiny said.

She liked discoveries. You could keep finding new ones all the time.

And then she wrote her biggest discovery.

She drew a big red arrow. She wrote: SURPRIZE!

Everyone followed her down the hall.

Jake the Sweeper was leaning on his broom. It was the first time Destiny had ever seen him smile.

She smiled, too.

Destiny put her finger to her lips. She opened the mop closet door.

"No more Terrible Thomas," Destiny whispered. "It's Mrs. Thomas."

The cat looked up at her.

Together everyone counted. Six kittens.

Destiny leaned over. She gave Mrs. Thomas's head a pat.

Her discovery certainly was the most surprising!

"Koun!" she said.